5 Minute Christmas Stories

5 Minute Christmas Stories

LITTLE TIGER PRESS
London

Contents

HURRY, SANTA!
Julie Sykes & Tim Warnes

9

THE VERY SNOWY CHRISTMAS
Diana Hendry & Jane Chapman

37

THE MAGICAL SNOWMAN
Catherine Walters & Alison Edgson

65

THE FIRST SNOW
M Christina Butler & Frank Endersby

93

ONE WINTER'S NIGHT
Claire Freedman & Simon Mendez

117

A CHRISTMAS WISH
Julia Hubery & Sophy Williams

145

ON THIS SPECIAL NIGHT
Claire Freedman & Simon Mendez

173

ONE MAGICAL CHRISTMAS
Alice Wood

201

THE GIFT OF CHRISTMAS
Christine Leeson & Gaby Hansen

229

SHHH!
Julie Sykes & Tim Warnes

257

8

Hurry, Santa!

Julie Sykes

Tim Warnes

It was Christmas Eve, and Santa's
busiest time of year.

"Wake up!" squeaked Santa's little
mouse. "Hurry, Santa! You mustn't
be late tonight."

"Goodness!" cried Santa. "Is that
the time? My alarm clock didn't
go off and I've overslept."

Santa leaped out of bed and began to pull
on his clothes. He was in such a hurry that
he put both feet down one trouser leg and
fell flat on his face.

"Hurry, Santa!" miaowed his cat. "You mustn't be late delivering the presents."

"You're right," agreed Santa, struggling up.

Santa hurried outside to his sleigh and picked up the reindeer harness.

"Oh no!" cried Santa. "Where are the reindeer?"

"They're loose in the woods," called Fox.
"Hurry, Santa! You mustn't be late tonight."
"You're right," said Santa.

Deep in the woods the reindeer
were having a snowball fight.
"Aaaaah!" cried Santa loudly,
as a snowball hit him in the face.

"Hurry, Santa," hooted Owl.
"You haven't got time to play
in the snow."

"I wasn't playing!" said Santa.
"Come on, you naughty reindeer.
We've got work to do."

17

At last Santa was ready to leave. With
a crack of his whip and a jingle of bells
he steered the sleigh towards the moon.
"Go, Reindeer, go!" he cried.

Around the world they flew, delivering presents to every child, until Santa turned the sleigh down towards a farm.

"Hurry, Santa!" called the reindeer. "The night's nearly over."

"I'm doing my best," said Santa, flicking the reins.

The reindeer quickened their pace.

"Whoa," Santa cried, but it was too late.

The sleigh skidded crazily across the snow.

"Ooooh deeeaaar!" cried Santa in alarm.

CRASH!

The sleigh came to rest in a ditch.

Santa scrambled to his feet and rubbed his bruised bottom. "Nothing broken," he boomed. "But we must hurry!"

When the reindeer had untangled themselves, everyone tugged and pulled and pushed as hard as they could, but the sleigh was completely stuck.

"It's no good," wailed the reindeer.
"We must keep trying," said Santa. "The sky
is getting lighter and we're running out of time."

Just then a loud neigh made Santa jump in surprise.
Trotting towards him was a very large horse.

"Hurry, Santa!" she neighed.

Everyone pulled together again, but the sleigh
was still stuck.

"Hurry, Santa!" called the cockerel from the gate.
"You must be quick. It's nearly morning."

"I must deliver the last of the presents on time,"
puffed Santa.

Then suddenly the sleigh began to move . . .

. . . and Santa fell backwards, cheering.

"Hurry, Santa!" called all the animals.

"You must be on your way before the

children wake up."

"You're right," agreed Santa.
"It's nearly Christmas Day!"

27

It was a close thing, but by dawn Santa
had managed to deliver every present.
"We did it!" yawned Santa.

But then Santa stared down at his
sack. There was still one present left.
"Oh no, how awful!" he cried.
"I've forgotten someone!"

29

Then Santa noticed that the animals
were laughing.

"That present is for you. It's from all of us,"
said the reindeer.

"Hurry, Santa!" added Santa's little mouse.

"You must open your present. It's Christmas Day!"

"You're right," chuckled Santa. "Now,

I wonder what it is . . ."

The Very Snowy Christmas

Diana Hendry   Jane Chapman

It was Christmas Eve.
Big Mouse was making
cheese pies. Little Mouse
was making paper chains.

"Happy Christmas to us!"
sang Little Mouse. "Big
Mouse, can I decorate
the Christmas tree now?
Can I? Can I?"

39

"We'll do it together," said Big Mouse.
Little Mouse hung golden acorns and
mistletoe berries on the tree. Big Mouse
put a star on the top.

"But we've forgotten the holly!" cried
Little Mouse. "I'll go and get some."
And off he rushed.

"Mind it has nice red berries!"
called Big Mouse.

Little Mouse set off down the path singing, "Jolly holly! Holly jolly! Jolly holly Christmas!"

But there was no holly to
be seen on the first corner.

And no holly on
the second corner.

And no holly on
the third corner.

44

Over the bridge ran
Little Mouse and at last
he found a holly bush with
shiny red berries. He jumped
up and down with excitement.

"Oh jolly holly! Holly jolly!
Jolly holly Christmas!" sang
Little Mouse, stretching high
on his toes to reach some.

But suddenly soft white flakes started falling all
round him. One flake fell on Little Mouse's nose
and made him sneeze. "Goodness me!" said
Little Mouse. "The sky is coming undone!"

Little Mouse began to hurry home. Lots more pieces of sky were falling on him. Faster and faster they fell. They fell on his ears and his whiskers and his tail. "Oh dear, oh dear," said Little Mouse, "I'd better take some of this to show Big Mouse. He'll know how to stitch the sky together again."

Little Mouse made a ball of white flakes and put it in his bucket. Back over the bridge he hurried.

Suddenly he saw a strange creature
in the water, making faces at him.
It had lots of ears and a squiffy face,
and it waved its arms at Little Mouse.

"Ooooh!" squeaked Little Mouse.
"It's a Mouse Ness Monster!"
And he fell on his bottom.

"Oh, I wish Big Mouse was here!"
he cried, scrambling up.

Back down the path ran Little Mouse,
looking over his shoulder to see if the
Mouse Ness Monster was following him.

It wasn't . . . but something was!
Little Mouse could see its paw prints
coming after him.

"EEEEKKK! HELP! EEEEKKK!"
squeaked Little Mouse. "Now there's
an Invisible Monster chasing me!"

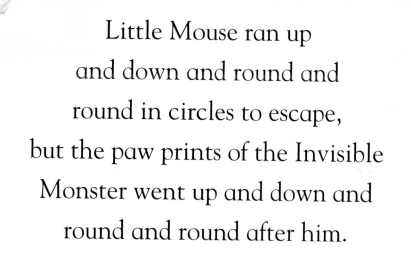

Little Mouse ran up
and down and round and
round in circles to escape,
but the paw prints of the Invisible
Monster went up and down and
round and round after him.

Little Mouse ran and ran.
Faster and faster whirled
the white flakes and faster
and faster ran Little Mouse.
And still the Invisible
Monster followed him.

At last Little Mouse saw
his house. But there in the
garden was a huge White Mouse!
"Oh no, no, no!" squeaked Little
Mouse. "Not another monster!"
Little Mouse trembled
and began to cry.

But then the front door
opened and there was
Big Mouse. Little
Mouse leaped into
Big Mouse's arms.

"Big Mouse, Big Mouse," he cried,
"the sky has come undone! And look!"
he wailed, pointing to the paw prints.
"An Invisible Monster has been
following me, and there was a
terrible Mouse Ness Monster in
the water, and now that scary
White Mouse is staring at me!"

57

"Oh, Little Mouse," said Big Mouse,
"the sky hasn't come undone.
  It's SNOWING!

"And there aren't any
  Invisible Monsters.
  Those are your paw prints.

"And that Mouse Ness
  Monster was your reflection
  in the water. Look!

"And this is a snow mouse I made to welcome you home," he said. "Let's make another." And so they did!

"Snow is magic!" cried Little Mouse.
"Yes," said Big Mouse. "Father Christmas likes snow too!"
Little Mouse jumped up and down. "Will he be here soon? Can I hang up my stocking now?"
"You can," said Big Mouse. "Let's go and get warm first."

So in they went and warmed
their paws by the fire.

Little Mouse and Big Mouse
hung up their stockings. The holly
berries shone in the firelight.

"It's almost Christmas," said
Little Mouse. "Jolly holly! Holly
jolly! Jolly holly Christmas!"
And he wriggled his warm toes.

The Magical Snowman

Catherine Walters

Alison Edgson

It was a clear, sparkling winter's day and Little Rabbit had been busy all morning.

"That's a lovely snowman," said Daddy. "Could you finish it later though? I need you to find some berries for our tea."

"Snowman will be sad if I leave him now," Little Rabbit said.

"He'll be fine," said Daddy gently. "He is just a snowman. He isn't real."

"He *is* real!" said Little Rabbit. "He's my friend!"

Daddy smiled as he gave Little Rabbit a kiss. "Don't go too far," he said.

"I won't!" said Little Rabbit.

Little Rabbit sang as he skipped
down the lane. Soon his paws were
sticky with purple juice.

Little Rabbit was
having so much fun . . .

he hardly noticed the
snow begin to fall.

A robin flitted ahead of
him and he followed it . . .

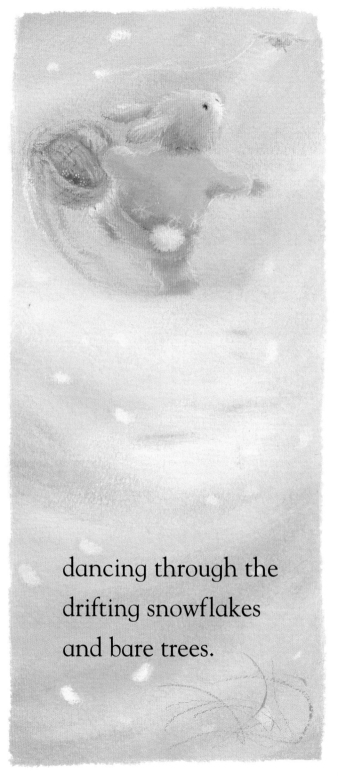

dancing through the
drifting snowflakes
and bare trees.

Then the robin flew away. Little Rabbit
stopped and looked around. He wasn't
sure which way he had come. The swirling
snow made everything look strange.

"How will I get home?" he cried.

Just then, a soft light sparkled through the trees. Smiling through the falling snow was his very own Snowman!

"Oh, Snowman," sighed Little Rabbit,
"I was all on my own."
   "Not all alone," smiled Snowman.
"I am always here for you, little friend."

Snowman dusted flakes from
Little Rabbit's fur and lifted
him onto his shoulders.
"I'll take you home," he
said. "Hold on tight!"

They whizzed down the hill . . .

WHOOOOOOOOOSH!

and landed in a snowy heap
by a frozen stream.

"Here we go!" Snowman laughed.
The world whisked by in a
shimmer of silver frost. It felt as
if they were flying.
"I'm coming home, Daddy!"
Little Rabbit called.

WHEEEEEEEEEEEE!

81

Suddenly, Snowman skidded to a halt at
the bottom of a hill.

"We'll have to walk now," he said, as
he swung Little Rabbit into his soft arms.

"Are we nearly there yet?" yawned
Little Rabbit.

"Not far now," said Snowman.

Meanwhile, Daddy Rabbit was hurrying through the whirling snow. He was very worried and he shivered in the icy wind.

"Little Rabbit!" he called. "Little Rabbit! Where are you?"

"Daddy!" cried Little Rabbit, when he heard his call. He leaped from Snowman's arms and bounded up the garden.

Daddy Rabbit hugged him tight.

"Thank goodness you're safe!" he said.

"I was so worried about you, all alone."

"I wasn't alone," said Little Rabbit. "Snowman
took care of me."

"Oh did he now?" Daddy chuckled.

Little Rabbit smiled. And Snowman smiled too.

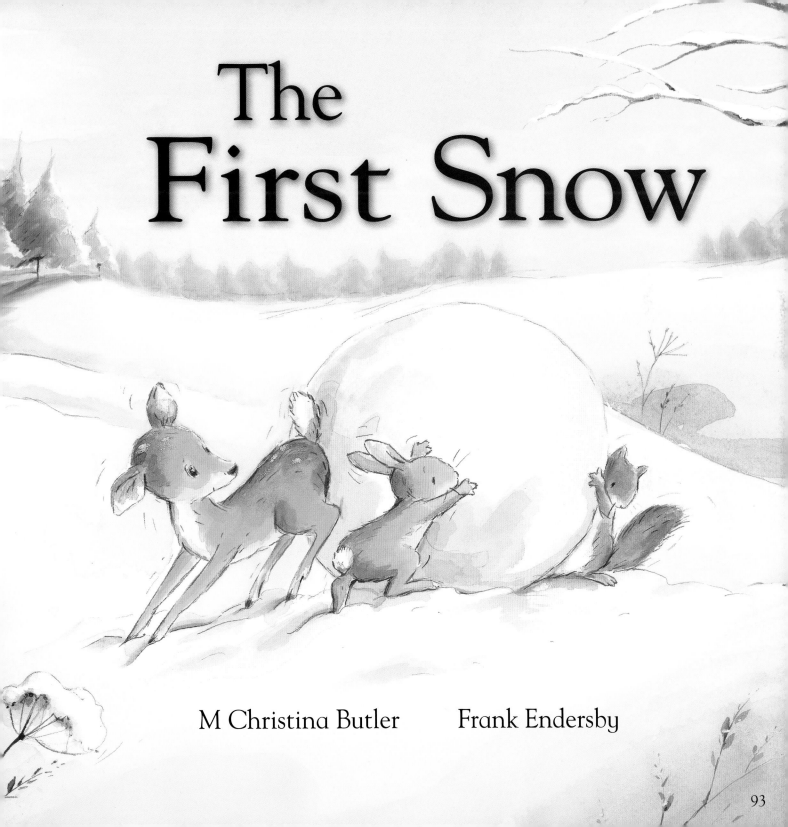

The First Snow

M Christina Butler   Frank Endersby

Little Deer peeped out of his bed and blinked in the morning sunshine. Everywhere looked different. The wood was covered with a huge white blanket.

Deer sniffed the sparkling ground
in front of him. "It's cold!" he cried.

Rabbit and Squirrel came skidding up to
Little Deer. "Snow! Snow! Look at the
snow!" they cheered.

"What's happened?" squeaked Deer. "Where's all the grass gone?"

Rabbit giggled and began to dig. "Ta-daah!" he said as a tuft of icy grass appeared.

Little Deer nibbled a bit of the cold, crispy grass. It was very strange.

"Catch me if you can!" cried Rabbit, skipping off.

"Easy peasy," laughed Squirrel. "Come on, Little Deer!"

Deer stepped carefully into the cold, slippery snow . . .

BUMP!

He slipped and slid and landed on his bottom! He tried to get up again and . . .

BUMP!
THUMP!

He fell on his nose in a snowdrift!

"Ow-ooh!" he cried.
"I HATE the snow!
I want to go home!"

"Don't go, Little Deer," said Rabbit.

"We're going to build a snowman!" said Squirrel.

"And we can't do it without you," added Rabbit.

So Rabbit made a
snowball and they
all began to push.

Slowly it got bigger
and bigger . . .

and soon it was so big
they couldn't push it
any further!

"Let's make the snowman a head!" said Squirrel.
But with a creak and a groan the snowball
began to roll down the hillside.
"Oh no!" shouted Deer. "Stop that snowman!"

Slipping and sliding, they all chased
down the hill. Faster and faster the
snowball rolled, and faster and faster
they tumbled after it . . .

SWOOSH! They skimmed off the bottom of the hillside, spun across the ice and landed, CRASH! in a big, snowy heap.

"That was awesome!" gasped Little Deer, as they all shook off the snow.

Slowly and slippily, wibbling and wobbling, they tried to stand up . . .
BUMP!

SWOOSH!

THUMP!
They skidded and slipped, and down they fell again!
"Bother!" squeaked Squirrel.
"Eeek!" giggled Rabbit.

"Hurray!" shouted Little Deer,
up on his feet at last. "Let's skate!"

On and on they twirled until the moon shone bright, and stars twinkled in the deep blue sky. Little Deer's first snow had been such a surprise, but it had been the best fun ever!

One Winter's Night

Claire Freedman   Simon Mendez

It was deepest, darkest winter. Wild snow blizzards had howled through the woods for days and the animals had been hiding in their dens, cold and hungry.

But tonight, suddenly, all was quiet
and the sky was clear.

Fox peeped from his snowy den. Out
of the darkness appeared a lone figure,
a badger, gleaming silver in the moonlight.

"Please," Badger called gently, "I'm so hungry. Do you have any food to share?"

Fox had hardly enough food for himself. But there was such a kind look in Badger's eyes. Fox felt he had to help him.

"Wait here," he said.

"Thank you," Badger smiled, gratefully taking the few berries Fox offered. Then off Badger went into the snow, head bent against the bitter wind.

Mouse was much too cold and hungry to sleep.
Suddenly she heard footsteps. "My, oh my!"
she gasped. "Who's out at this time of night?"

"Hello!" a silvery figure called softly.

"I'm very hungry. Do you have any spare food?"

"I've nothing at all!" Mouse grumbled.

"I understand," Badger said, and turned to go.

Mouse listened as the heavy crunch of
Badger's footsteps slowly faded. Badger
had seemed so gentle.

"Wait!" Mouse scampered after him.
"Hare lives nearby. Maybe she can help!"

Together, Mouse and
Badger struggled to
Hare's house.

Even in the dark,
Mouse felt safe beside
Badger, his warm eyes
twinkling like bright stars.

Hare was rather cross to be woken up. And she didn't have much to share with anyone!

"I know it's late, Hare, but I told Badger you might help," Mouse whispered. "We're freezing cold and starving."

"I suppose you had both better come in then," said Hare.

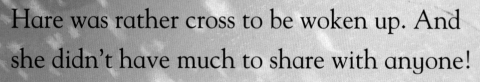

Mouse, Hare and
Badger nibbled
on Hare's last
few berries.

All too soon, Badger
thanked them and left.
Without him the burrow
felt colder, and the
night darker.

"Poor Badger – it's freezing outside!"
Mouse sighed.

"I hope he'll be all right," said Hare.
Just then they spotted a shadowy
figure moving slowly towards them . . .

"It's Fox!" cried Mouse.

"What are you doing here?"
Hare asked him.

"I'm searching for Badger!"
Fox explained. "He was so
tired and hungry!"

"I think we should go and
look for him," Mouse said.

In the shimmering snow, Badger's
footprints were pools of silver.

The blizzard blew stronger as the
friends followed Badger's tracks
deeper and deeper into the woods.
"Over there!" cried Fox at last.

Badger was asleep, covered
in a frosting of snow.
"Poor Badger!" Fox cried.

Mouse and Hare
gathered some soft
leaves for Badger's bed.
Fox dug a snowy shelter
to keep him snug.

Then together they curled
up cosy and warm in
their snowy den.

The next morning Badger had gone!
"I wonder if Badger will ever visit us
again?" said Fox.

But just then, Mouse gave
an excited shout. "Look!
Over there!"

Everyone stared in surprise.

"It's a gift from Badger!" Fox gasped.
Mouse read the tiny message:

In every caring thing you do,
The love you give comes back to you!

"We all knew he was special!" Hare cried.
Suddenly the sun burst through the clouds
and a million snowflakes sparkled –
bright as the twinkle in Badger's eyes!

A Christmas Wish

Julia Hubery

Sophy Williams

Gemma gazed up at the Christmas
tree and breathed in the magical
smell of Christmas.

At last it was time to unpack
the decorations.

Gemma's brother Ty danced round her knees impatiently.

"Ty, calm down or you'll POP!" she laughed.

Gemma told him all about the shiny baubles, the glittering tinsel and, her favourite, the leaping snow deer.

One by one – oh so carefully – Gemma unwrapped the decorations.

At last she found the dusty box where the snow
deer slept. Ty reached out for the sparkly deer.
"Careful, Ty! Don't touch!" cried Gemma,
yanking the box away quickly – too quickly.
The snow deer fell from his hands . . .

151

There was the tiniest
snap as it hit the floor,
and lay broken.

"What's happened?" asked Mum.

"It's the snow deer, the one I really love," replied Gemma. "Stupid Ty broke him to bits."

"It was an accident, Gem. You know how excited he is," said Mum.

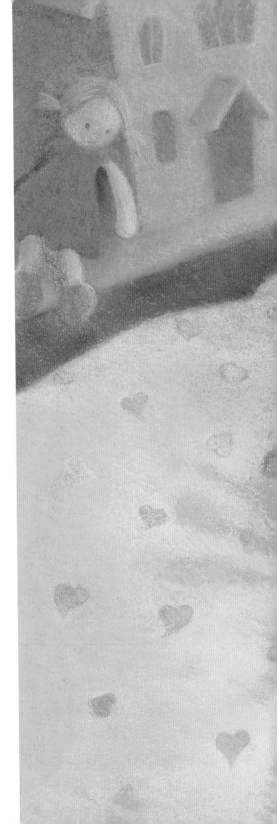

Ty tried to say sorry. He brought his favourite teddy to Gemma.

But Gemma wouldn't look at Ty. She stomped out of the room.

Gemma laid the snow deer on her pillow.
She remembered last Christmas: dark evenings,
sitting by the tree, dreaming with the snow deer . . .

. . . dreams where he carried her
through sparkling skies, high above
sleepy toy-town cities and patchwork fields . . .

. . . then higher still, to the North Pole. In crystal palaces shimmering with the light of a thousand fairies, they danced and spun and whirled till even the stars fell asleep.

"Ty would have loved flying with the snow deer," thought Gemma. She remembered last Christmas Eve, when he had bounced into her room and snuggled up with her like a big teddy bear.

Gemma began to feel she'd
been mean to Ty.

When Gemma opened
her door, she nearly fell
over something.

On the floor was a
badly-wrapped parcel,
and a little card with
a big wobbly "sorry".

Inside was a pot of glue.

"To mend the snow deer!"
Gemma laughed.

Gemma crept downstairs.

"Look what Ty gave me," she whispered.

Working patiently, Mum and Gemma
stuck the snow deer back together.

"Now, it really is bedtime," said Mum.
But Gemma had one more thing to do.
She took the snow deer into Ty's room . . .

"Ty," she whispered, "the snow deer's better now. Let's make a Christmas wish. Maybe he'll fly us to the stars."

Moonbeams kissed their sleepy heads as they closed their eyes tight and wished . . .

. . . and together they flew high
above the sleepy towns into
the magical, velvet night.

On This
Special
Night

Claire Freedman   Simon Mendez

It was a silent winter's night. Frosty trees glistened in the shadowy twilight. The heavens sparkled, watching, watching . . .

Little Kitten was snuggled up in the old, wooden barn. Outside, stars studded the inky-blue sky.

"Try and go to sleep," Mother Cat said.

"But the stars are so bright tonight," cried Little Kitten.

One star was bigger than the rest. Blazing with a brilliant light, it seemed to fill the heavens.

"That must be a special star," Mother Cat said.

Just at that moment, a gentle crackle of leaves broke through the stillness of the night.

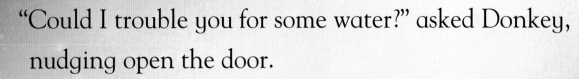

"Could I trouble you for some water?" asked Donkey, nudging open the door.

"Of course," said Mother Cat kindly.

"Thank you," Donkey smiled. "I am on a special journey tonight." And he trundled out again into the silver moonlight.

Little Kitten watched, wondering . . .

Just then Little Kitten heard a gentle *Baa! Baa!*
"I've walked such a long way," bleated Lamb.
"Could I rest for a while in your comfy hay?"
"Why, of course," Mother Cat smiled.

Outside, high in the sky, the biggest, brightest star blazed on, watching, waiting . . . "Do you know why that star is so bright tonight?" Little Kitten asked Lamb.

"Oh yes!" whispered Lamb. "I can
tell you a story about that star . . ."

183

But before Lamb could begin, there came a
Scritch! Scratch! Scritch! Scratch! and three tiny
mice peered through a crack in the wall.

"May we come in?" they shivered. "We've
been walking forever, and our paws are frozen!"

"It's time I carried on my journey," Lamb said.
And silently he tiptoed away.

The mice nestled down, sharing
the shelter of the snug, cosy bed.

"Are you following the star?"
Little Kitten asked.

But before they could answer,
there came a *Moo! Moooo!* and
Calf peeped his head round the
battered door.

"Do you have any food?"
Calf asked.

"Please have some fresh hay," said Mother Cat.
"Thank you," said Calf. "I can't stay long;
I must be on my way."
"We must hurry too,"
the mice said.

189

"Tonight is a very special night,"
Calf said. "Something amazing is
going to happen."

"Can we go too?" begged Little Kitten.

But it was very late, so Mother Cat
and Little Kitten climbed to the top of
the barn roof to see what they could see.

Little Kitten gazed in wonder at the
sparkling, starlit sky. It felt as if the whole
world were holding its breath, watching, waiting . . .

"Look, Mummy!" Little Kitten cried.
In the distance were three magnificent camels.

"This is a very special night!" Mother Cat whispered.
"Come on, Little Kitten. Let's go and see what's happening."

Shadows softened in the still night air as Mother Cat and Little Kitten reached the bottom of the hill. There stood a simple stable, aglow in the light of the shining star.

Tenderly, Mother Cat helped Little Kitten
squeeze inside. His heart burst with happiness
at what he saw: a baby! It was sleeping soundly
in the sweet, soft hay.

This was a very special baby.
    The animals watched quietly as above
them the bright, bright star blazed in the night . . .
shining with peace
                and joy
                        and love.

One Magical Christmas

Alice Wood

It was Christmas Eve in the workshop and
Father Christmas was loading up the sleigh.

Teddy was worried. "Do you think we'll like
our new home?" he asked.

"Of course we will!" said Dolly. "It will be wonderful!"

At last the sleigh was full and they were
on their way! Dolly and Teddy peered over
the edge as they flew up, up into the night sky.
But then Teddy's scarf caught in the wind and
whipped away into the night.

"Oh no!" he gasped.

As soon as they had landed, he leaped down and raced after it.

"Come back, Teddy! Come back!" cried Dolly. "Father Christmas will be leaving again soon!"

But Teddy didn't stop.
He chased, jumped and
reached out his paws until
at last he caught the scarf.

"Quick, Teddy!" said Dolly,
and they hurried back
towards the sleigh.

But the sleigh had left without them.

"Father Christmas! Stop! Come back!"
they cried.

But it was too late. They were all alone
in the strange, dark woods.

"Oh no!" sobbed Teddy.
"What are we going to do now?"
Dolly gave him a cuddle.

"We'll have to catch up
with Father Christmas,"
she said, bravely.

So they set off across
the snow together.
It was hard work.

They were only small,
and everything around
them was so big.

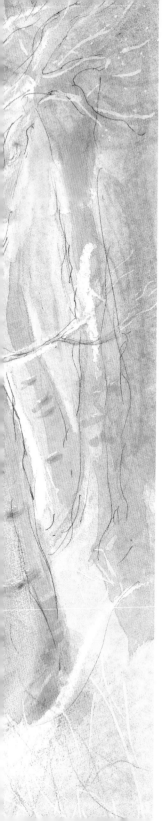

As they walked along, something tickled Teddy's nose.

"Oh, Dolly!" he giggled. "It's snowing!"

Dolly tried to catch the fluffy snowflakes on her tongue. Teddy built a snow bear.

"Come on," Dolly said after a while, "we need to keep going."

It was getting very late. The snow fell thicker.
The sky grew darker. The wind blew harder.
Dolly and Teddy struggled along in the
deep snow.

Suddenly, they heard a noise.

"What was that?" whispered Teddy, holding on to Dolly tightly.

They looked up and saw a dark shape in the tall trees . . .

Whooo!

Whooo!

WHOOO!

215

"Run!" cried Dolly.

But then Teddy tripped at the top of a hill and tumbled all the way down.

"Oh, Teddy!" Dolly cried. "Are you all right?"

"I think so," he said. "Look!"

There, flickering through the trees, was a warm, glowing light.

"It's a house!" said Dolly.

The house looked so warm and inviting.
There was a big Christmas tree with
fairy lights all over it.

"Let's go in," said Dolly. "I'm sure
Father Christmas will find us here."

Dolly and Teddy crept into the house, to the room with the twinkling Christmas tree. Under the tree they found two little beds, so they snuggled down to rest.

"Will we *ever* find our new home?" asked Teddy.

"Of course we will!" said Dolly, and they soon fell sound asleep.

In the middle of the night,
Father Christmas arrived at the
house on the edge of the woods.
When he found the two little toys
asleep in the two little stockings, he
could not believe his eyes.
"How did you two get here?"
he wondered. "Well, well,
well. You've found your
new home all on your
own! It must be
**Christmas
magic.**"

On Christmas morning, two little children raced downstairs to see what Father Christmas had brought them. Under the tree they found just what they had wished for – a cuddly teddy and a beautiful dolly!

Dolly and Teddy had found their new home all on their own. And it really was wonderful!

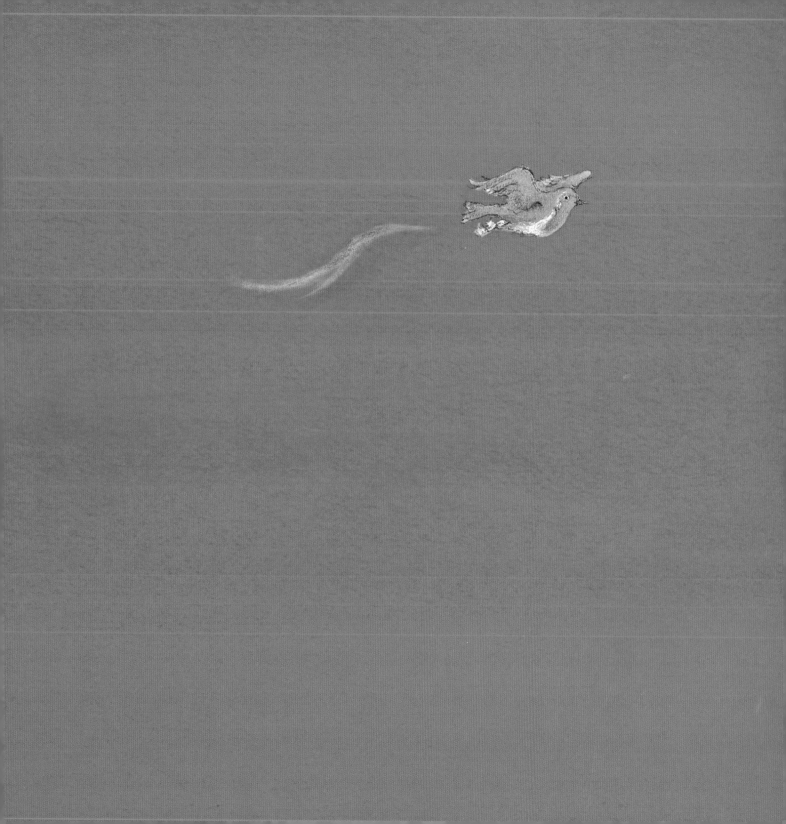

The Gift of Christmas

Christine Leeson

Gaby Hansen

It was Molly Mouse's first Christmas. The sky was streaked with pink and gold, and there was a tingle in the air.

Through the window of a house a giant Christmas tree shone and glittered in the night.

"I wish we had a Christmas tree," sighed Molly.

"Why not go into the woods to find one?" said her mum. "You could make it look just as pretty as that."

"That's a good idea!" said Molly.
She called her brothers and sisters,
and off they all scampered.

First they came to a barn. The
mice rummaged through it, looking
for something to add to their tree.

Molly found a doll under a big
pile of hay. "This is just right,"
she said.

"Hold it!" said the old farm dog. "That's mine!"

"Don't chase us!" cried Molly. "I only thought the doll would be nice for our Christmas tree."

The old dog yawned. And because it was Christmas, he said the mice could borrow his toy.

The mice thanked the dog and left the farmyard.

"Hey, I've found something else!" Molly shouted.

It was a golden ribbon, hanging from a branch
of an oak tree. Molly scampered up the trunk,
took hold of the ribbon and pulled . . .

237

But the ribbon belonged to a magpie.
She had taken it to line her nest.
"I only wanted something for our
Christmas tree," pleaded Molly.

Now usually the magpie chased mice. But because
it was Christmas, she let go of the ribbon and
Molly took it away.

In the distance Molly saw some red shiny things
lying on the ground. They were like the balls
on the Christmas tree in the window.

"Perfect!" cried Molly. "Now we
have a doll, a golden ribbon and
a shiny ball!"

"Hey! That's my apple," a fox barked.

"We only thought it would look good on our Christmas tree," said Molly, trembling.

The fox sniffed. And because it was Christmas, he let Molly take the apple away.

Twilight was falling as the mice went deeper into the woods. There, in the middle of a bramble bush, they could see a lovely shining star and a dozen tiny lights glittering green and gold.

"Stars for our tree!" shouted Molly. But when she reached into the bush she found, not stars . . .

. . . but a collar, belonging to a mother cat.

"Oh dear!" gulped Molly. "I only wanted something sparkly for our Christmas tree."

The cat pricked her ears. But because it was Christmas, she slipped off her old collar and let the mice take it away.

At last, in a clearing in the very deepest part of the wood, the mice found a large green tree.

"Our Christmas tree!" cried Molly.

On its branches they hung the doll, the ribbon, the apple and the cat's collar.

"Oh," said Molly when they had finished. "It doesn't look a bit like the tree I saw." Sadly the mice walked slowly away and all the way home to bed.

249

In the middle of the night
Mother Mouse woke up
her little ones. "Come with me,"
she whispered. "I have something to show you."
The little mice scurried along behind their
mother, past the farm and into the woods.

At last the mice reached the clearing
where the green tree grew.

Molly's eyes grew round and shiny.
"Oh, look at that!" she cried.

During the night the animals had added more decorations to the tree. The little tree sparkled and shone, and even the stars seemed to be caught in its branches.

"Our tree is even better than the one in the window," whispered Molly, happily.

And all the animals nodded and smiled.

Shhh!

Julie Sykes   Tim Warnes

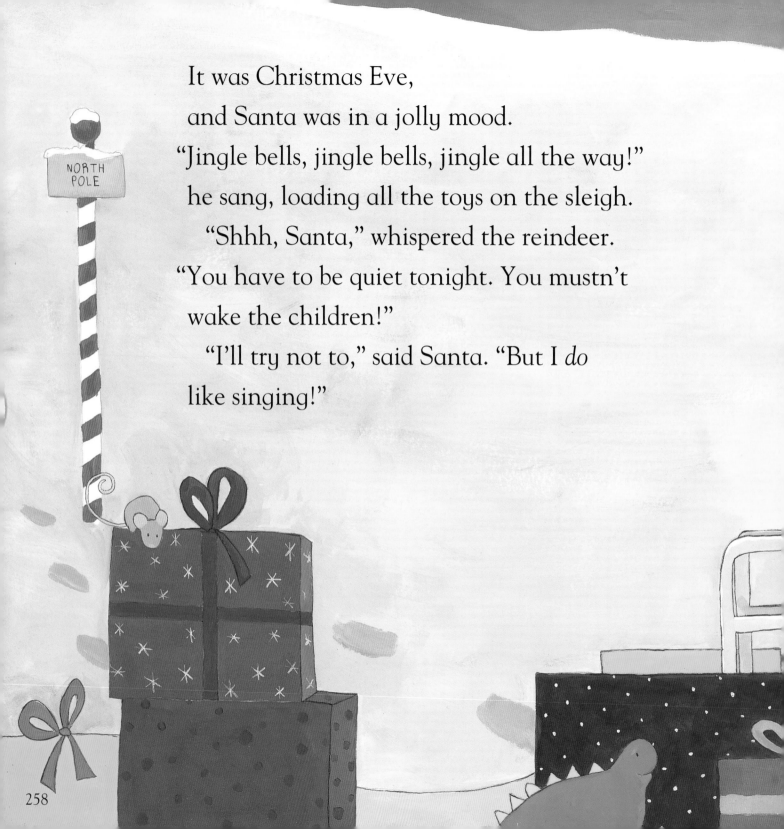

It was Christmas Eve,
and Santa was in a jolly mood.
"Jingle bells, jingle bells, jingle all the way!"
he sang, loading all the toys on the sleigh.
"Shhh, Santa," whispered the reindeer.
"You have to be quiet tonight. You mustn't
wake the children!"
"I'll try not to," said Santa. "But I *do*
like singing!"

Over the moonlit world they sped,
towards the sleeping children.

Santa was so excited that he forgot
to land on the roof of the first house.

261

Santa landed in the garden next
to a friendly cat.

"Happy Christmas, Cat!" he roared.

The cat waved her tail in the air.

"Shhh, Santa," she whispered. "You
mustn't wake the children!"

"Of course I won't," said Santa,
jumping out of the sleigh.

263

Santa threw his sack over his
shoulder and tiptoed along the
garden path towards the back door.

"OOH, OOH, OOH-OOPS!" cried
Santa, sliding on a patch of ice and
crashing to the ground.

"Shhh, Santa," whispered the snowman.
"You mustn't wake the children!"
    "Sorry," said Santa, picking himself up.
"But Christmas is my favourite time of year!"

When he reached the Christmas tree
Santa pulled some presents from his sack.

A jack-in-the-box burst open,
and made Santa jump in surprise.

"HEE, HEE, HEE," laughed Santa. "Shhh, Santa," whispered the family's dog. "You mustn't wake the children!"

"Mustn't wake the children," agreed Santa. He put his finger to his lips, and crept across the room . . .

. . . but he didn't notice the tinsel,
trailing all over the floor –
until it was too late.

"BUMPITY, BUMPITY,
BUMP!" boomed Santa,
landing on a roller skate.
He skidded across the carpet,
and fell headfirst into the
fireplace. It was a good job
the fire was out!

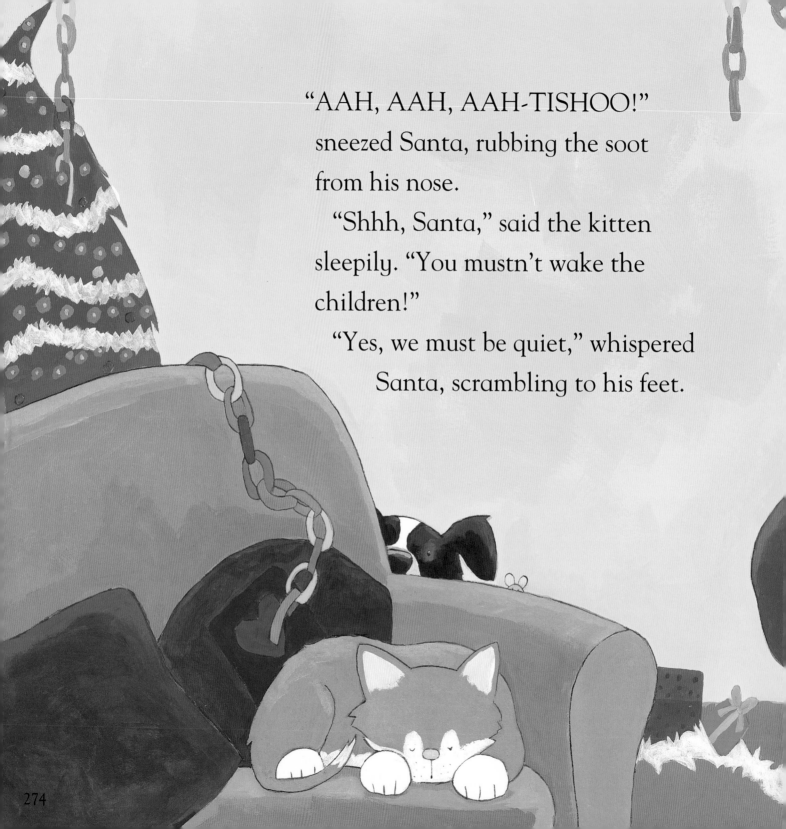

"AAH, AAH, AAH-TISHOO!"
sneezed Santa, rubbing the soot
from his nose.

"Shhh, Santa," said the kitten
sleepily. "You mustn't wake the
children!"

"Yes, we must be quiet," whispered
Santa, scrambling to his feet.

Santa picked up his sack and hurried back to his sleigh. There were lots more visits to make before Christmas Day. But at last his sack was empty.

Santa rubbed his eyes sleepily and called,
"Home, Reindeer!"

And with a toss of their heads and a jingle
of bells, the reindeer leaped into the sky.

"HO, HO, HO!" shouted Santa loudly.
"Here we are, home at last!" Then he
added quietly to himself, "Shhh, Santa,
I mustn't wake the children!"

It had been a busy night, and Santa
felt very tired. He made himself a cup of
hot cocoa, put on his slippers, lay back in
his armchair and fell fast asleep . . .

"... Z Z Z Z Z," snored Santa.

"MUNCH, MUNCH, CRUNCH!" went the reindeer, as they tucked into their supper.

"SHHH!" squeaked Santa's little mouse. "YOU MUSTN'T WAKE SANTA!"

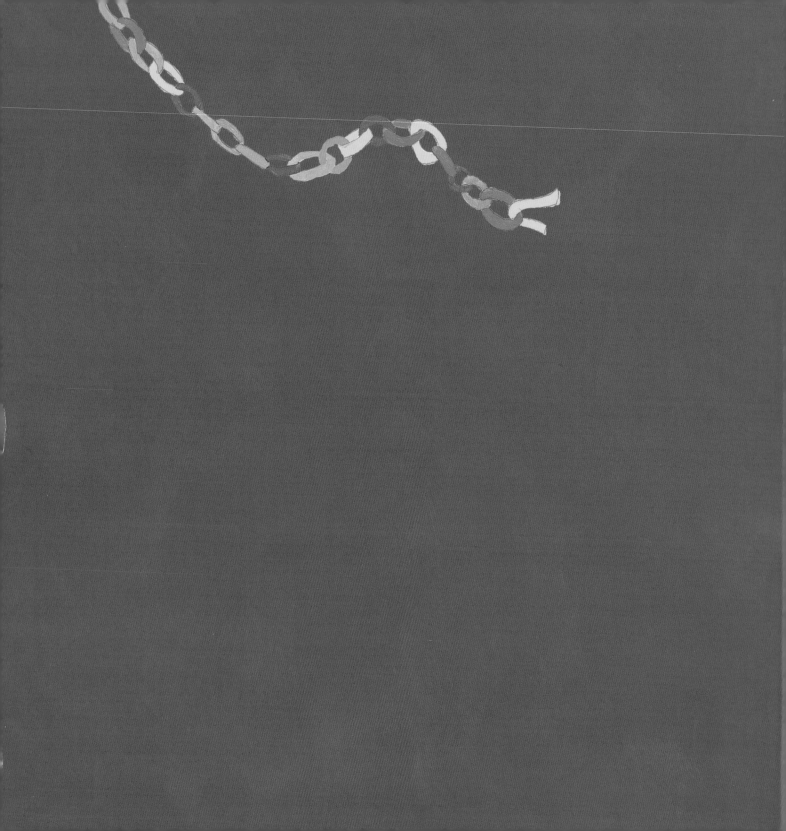

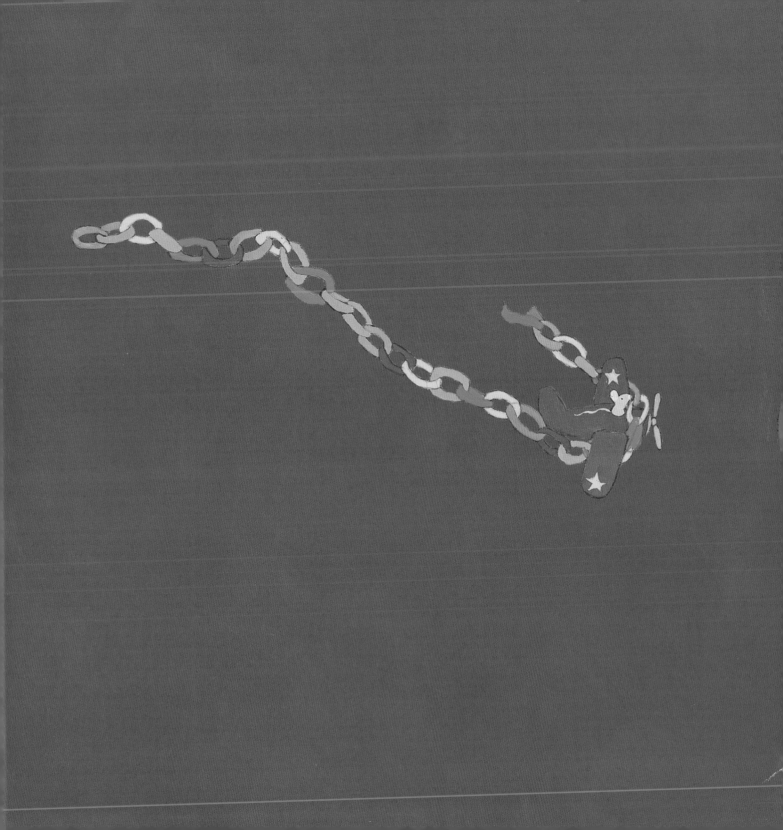

5 MINUTE CHRISTMAS STORIES

LITTLE TIGER PRESS
1 The Coda Centre,
189 Munster Road,
London, SW6 6AW
www.littletiger.co.uk

First published in Great Britain 2012
by Little Tiger Press, London
This edition published 2012

Printed in China • LTP/1900/1031/0814

ISBN 978-1-84895-552-3

4 6 8 10 9 7 5 3

HURRY, SANTA!

Julie Sykes
Illustrated by Tim Warnes

First published in Great Britain 1998
by Little Tiger Press

Text copyright © Julie Sykes 1998
Illustrations copyright © Tim Warnes 1998
Visit Tim Warnes at www.ChapmanandWarnes.com

THE VERY SNOWY CHRISTMAS

Diana Hendry
Illustrated by Jane Chapman

First published in Great Britain 2005
by Little Tiger Press

Text copyright © Diana Hendry 2005
Illustrations copyright © Jane Chapman 2005
Visit Jane Chapman at www.ChapmanandWarnes.com

THE MAGICAL SNOWMAN

Catherine Walters
Illustrated by Alison Edgson

First published in Great Britain 2009
by Little Tiger Press

Text copyright © Catherine Walters 2009
Illustrations copyright © Alison Edgson 2009

THE FIRST SNOW

M Christina Butler
Illustrated by Frank Endersby

First published in Great Britain 2010
by Little Tiger Press

Text copyright © M Christina Butler 2010
Illustrations copyright © Frank Endersby 2010

THE GIFT OF CHRISTMAS

Christine Leeson
Illustrated by Gaby Hansen

First published in Great Britain 2000
by Little Tiger Press

Text copyright © Christine Leeson 2000
Illustrations copyright © Gaby Hansen 2000

SHHH!

Julie Sykes
Illustrated by Tim Warnes

First published in Great Britain 1996
by Little Tiger Press

Text copyright © Julie Sykes 1996
Illustrations copyright © Tim Warnes 1996
Visit Tim Warnes at www.ChapmanandWarnes.com